Enough
To Die For

G. Lorna Hirschfield

A huge thank you to the most supportive, loving and considerate family in the world. Thank you for helping me achieve my dream. I couldn't have done it without your constant encouraging.

I love you all.

Table of Contents

Chapter 1

BANG, BANG, BANG! Three bullets danced through the air into his chest followed by a big thud of his lifeless body hitting the cold, indifferent ground. The heavy gun slipped out of her soft hands like sand running through her fingers. The air around her turned black, stiff and heavy as she realized what she had just done. She drew her attention away from the body she had just turned into a corpse to meet his eyes. "You! You did this! You made me this monster!" Addison's voice echoed through the cold, dark street as she stood above the slowly spreading pool of blood.

He stood across from her. His face was stiff. Talking to him was like talking to a brick wall. His blood-chilling grey eyes looked at her but stared straight through her. His curly black hair fell perfectly in front of his eyes, highlighting the occasional sparkle.

He had a permanent smirk stitched onto his face. Addison wore a dark grey pencil skirt with a pastel pink blouse hanging loosely. Her warm blond hair gathered into a messy bun which was now falling apart. Her sparkling, honest, blue eyes were now cloudy and lifeless. Her freckle painted cheeks were now tear-stained.

"Why?! Why couldn't you just leave me be? Why couldn't you just have turned away?!" Her voice that usually sounded like sweet honey was now bitter and cold.

Her mascara had stained her tears black. He took his hand out of his ripped black jeans and took off his leather jacket while moving close enough to Addison to make her lose her breath. He brushed her hair out of her face and placed his heavy jacket on her shoulders. Addison attempted to speak, but she was at a loss of words. He stepped back and said, "No point crying over spilt milk." Then silence came. He then moved his hand over to her face and wiped her tears. Enraged, Addison pushed him back. His smirk remained plastered onto his perfectly chiseled face. She pushed again and again, but he wouldn't move. She lifted her arms and attempted to punch him, but she was blocked by his arms catching hers.

"After everything, I don't know why I stay, I don't know why I don't just turn you in right now." Her voice breaks more with every word as she pulls her shaking arm back aggressively.
"I don't know why I don't just shoot you and end it all right here." Her tears weren't tears of sadness any more.

He leaned down and picked up the gun from the ground and wiped off the blood. "Here you go", he handed her the loaded gun. "Lucky you, one bullet left." His smirk grew greater than before.

He looked straight into her eyes. His eyes were on her and her eyes were on him as if the world had stopped.

One final BANG!

One final pulling of the trigger and the only noise remaining was the echoing silence which fell among the whole city. Many in her situation may think that this night would be the end, little did they know that this was only the beginning of a whole different world.

Addison wore grey sweatpants and a plain white tee as she flipped the pan of stir-fry, she had been trying to cook for the past two hours. "Did you see where I put the soy sauce?"

Addison asked the man sitting at the table opposite the kitchen counter while scanning the black counter tops. "Alex?" she said once again while looking at the huge mess she'd made. Countless packets of noodles were scattered all over. It was such a big mess she couldn't see anything. She turned around and at a glimpse at the sink she snapped. She'd been trying to cook for this man who never helps with anything. Not once had he tried to even offer to help or ask if she was okay. She'd had such a bad day at work. Her stupid boss cut her wage again. She worked countless hours every day at a job she couldn't stand and came home to this guy who can't take his eyes off his phone for three seconds. Her pathetic life infuriated her.

She turned to face him and saw him sitting on one chair and his legs up on the other. He had bright blue eyes and dark brown hair parted to one side. Alex was on his phone and ignored her. Nothing new there. They had met three years ago in Spain. Addison went on a trip with her mother to celebrate her graduating from university with a degree in business management. She'd spent three years of her life with this guy who didn't help or do anything that wouldn't benefit him directly. Yes, he had a pretty face, but was it really worth all this wasted time?

"Babe!" Addison's words bounced off the four walls of her small apartment and back into her own ears. "Alex, I've called you three times what are you doing?" She said louder this time returning to the stove. "Geez, chill don't have a

9

cow. What do you need?" he said momentarily looking up from his phone.

The white artificial light lit up his eyes more than Addison could ever. Addison's grip to the pan tightened and the anger flushed through her cheeks when all of a sudden, the pan set on fire. It was a bright fade of red, yellow and orange. It flowed confidently from the metal pan and Addison remained still admiring the dancing flames. "What the hell Addison?! What did you do?" Alex's attention was finally away from his phone. He jumped up. He wore a black and white lumberjack shirt partly tucked into acid-washed jeans. His ankle-high black Converse sneakers were tightly tied. "I didn't do anything, it just set on fire." Addison tried to prove her innocence. "Yeah sure because pans just set on fire," he said in sarcasm. He ran over to the pan and threw it into the sink. A colossal body of grey steam came rushing out of the sink clouding her small apartment.

"Well, that's just great." He said and paused.

"I'm starving and now you've burned the food." He added on. While walking over to the small high window above the dining room table and pushing it open.

"Maybe if you had done something apart from staring at your phone the whole time we're together, it wouldn't have happened." Addison snapped back. She'd had enough.

"Oh, so this is my fault. It's my fault that you burned our food because I'm meant to watch you like a two-year-old when you're cooking?" he said walking closer to him.

Addison looked at the overflowing garbage and found a way to make her escape. "I'm done fighting. The garbage is overflowing and it doesn't look like you're going to take it out, so I guess you should let the two-year-old do it." Addison stormed over to the bin and grabbed the garbage letting her bitter voice echo. With one hand holding the heavy black bag, Addison uses the other to push open the heavy, tall, grey door. The cold handle sends a shiver up her spine as

11

if something inside her knew walking out that door would be the mistake of a lifetime. Her white sneakers touched the Grey fuzzy carpet of the outside hallways. There were occasional lamps lighting up the lonely dark corners. She walked all the way to the elevator and turned right into the garbage room. She swung the heavy bag into the chute and pushed it down using her anger to fuel her strength while holding her breath trying to avoid the acrid, eye-watering, lingering smell. She pushed the door using her body and walked out of the room and finally let her breath out. Addison loved being alone. She could think about her life, about the past and future. She could escape from the present. She walked further down the hallway past the garbage chute into the main area of her floor. She leaned against the wall and slowly sunk down. In that time, she was alone, her thoughts rolled over her.

She thought about many things. She thought about her boyfriend, about how he ignores her and belittles her. She thought about her lonely mother, who'd never been the same since the divorce. She thought about the stars so far away in the sky and the freedom that they have. She even thought about those animals deep in the ocean, so far down that they would be forever protected from humanity. Time quickly passed, and she awoke from her daydream, she knew exactly what she had to do next. She was going to go back home and tell the guy who wasted three years of her life to get out of her apartment and never come back. She was determined and powered by the raging fury inside her, confidence flowed through her as she rose to her feet and dusted off her pants.

She was ready and could hear her heart in her ears. She quickly arrived at the intersection of hallways. As she began to turn to the left, she felt somehow, someone was trying to stop her from going any further. She shook off the weird feeling and turned left and ignored every warning.

She turned the last corner before reaching her apartment. Her apartment was one of the last ones before the next turn. As she walked out of the corner, she saw him. His eyes were the most beautiful piercing grey she'd ever seen. They were so full of life yet so dead and cold at the same time. His face, emotionless. He wore a white buttoned-up shirt. Not a single wrinkle. He had black dress pants on and a plain black tie. He had dark brown polished shoes. He was perfect. Everything about him was perfect.

Well, almost perfect. His right-hand index finger was wrapped around a steel trigger. The gun was heavy and fully loaded, but he held it like a feather, like a glove molded to his hand. He was a man who did not believe in mercy.

"I... I promise you I can stop it. I can stop them." The man cowering opposite him had dark blond hair and light brown eyes filled with fear which could be smelt from miles away.

"Please don't..." Bang! It seemed absurd to her that such a small movement of a finger could end a person's life so easily.

Addison gasped and that was all that she needed to do to blow her cover. "What do we have here?" His masculine, deep voice laced with his British accent was the cherry on top of all his twisted perfection.

The stranger seemed intrigued by Addison. He had a smirk on his face. His white shirt was now splattered with blood. "Don't hurt me!" Addison burst out to save herself. The words flowed from her mouth as if she'd acted on an impulse.

"Don't hurt you? Love, I wouldn't dream of it" He said letting his smirk turn into a smile right before lifting his gun to eye level.

Addison instinctively started to run and just as she dived around the corner of the hallway, he pulled the trigger. The heavy bullet smashed into the wall near her head. He turned around and picked up his dark blazer. He ran his fingers through his hair and looked up to the camera. He smiled and said "Not tonight." He then put a bullet through the CCTV camera and continued walking, leaving Addison behind without even a glance at the dead man silently crumpled in the hallway. His actions left Addison wishing she'd never left her apartment.

A fellow human, begging for his or her life meant nothing to him. He was a trained, ruthless killer who had the blood of thousands on his hands. Addison was not about to be an exception. Just as Addison dove past the corner, he had fired the gun. If Addison had managed to keep her mouth closed, maybe just maybe he would have let her live. Addison pressed back against the wall breathing heavily. She felt like she was drowning as she stared at the bullet that had fallen to the floor beside her unsteady hand.

At that moment time froze. She couldn't breathe. Her mind tried to process so many things. She'd been shot at. She'd witnessed a murder. Less than 24 hours ago she was okay. She curled up into a ball and stayed there in a trance. After what seemed an eternity, she was awoken by Alex screaming her name. He wore the same outfit but had his car keys in his left hand and his thick winter jacket on.

"Addison!" Alex's voice echoed through her head, but she still couldn't move.

Alex lifted her into his arms and carried her back into her apartment and put her into her bed. The next thing Addison can recall was seeing her boyfriend sitting on the edge of her bed staring at her as if she was some type of alien. "Get out!" she shouted so loud the whole building seemed to shake. "Addison, calm down I'm only trying to help you. I heard gunshots." He said, trying to calm her down. "You heard gunshots? That's why you're rushed out so quick?" She said sarcastically while looking around her bedroom in a panic. Her head was spinning.

"Addison don't be like that. What would we do if I also died? Who would save you?" Alex tried to defend his actions. "Alex, I'm exhausted. I'm tired and have no energy for this anymore. Three years with you have managed to drain everything I've had. It's over now please don't make me ask again, get out!" She said staring straight into his dark lifeless soul.

"Common Adi, you don't mean that we both know that." He said but Addison wasn't having it. Addison got out of the bed and asked once more for him to leave. He refused to be kicked out but Addison had enough of his ways. Still determined from earlier She stared at him in the eye. She pushed him so hard he fell.

"I recall telling you to get out." Alex rose to his feet and cracked his neck. "Oh, you just messed up big," he said while cracking his knuckles.

Alex threw the first punch and knocked her to the ground. Little did he know that he, in fact, was the one who messed up big time. With her hand on her eye, Addison got up and looked him up and down as a smirk spread across her bruising face. "Is that all you can do?" She said challenging him. He threw more and she dodged them easily. She felt pretty grateful to the kickboxing classes her grandfather had made her take back all those years ago.

She then mocked him by yawning.

"Ha, you save me?!" She said before finally seeing an opening and punching back hard, leaving a tingling sensation spreading through her right wrist.

"I'll tell you what, you get out and maybe just maybe I'll let you be." Alex was having trouble staying on his feet now and looked around frightened before he finally ran out.

Addison gathered herself and did her breathing exercises to calm down. She walked over to her kitchen feeling her cold tiled floor on her bare feet and pain in her right hand. She opened her bright white freezer and took out an ice pack. She placed it on her eye and winced. "It was so worth it." She said to herself. While grinning.

While holding the cold ice pack on her bruised eye, she walked over to her couch and grabbed the remote from the wooden end table. She clicked the power button and began watching her favorite TV show. "Just tell her you love her already!" She shouted at the TV.

Above her, she could hear the constant moving of furniture. She could hear people banging and jumping above her. Considering the day, she'd already had she wasn't about to let her neighbor make it any worse. She paused her TV show and walked into the storage room, grabbed her broom and began banging on the ceiling. "There are people below you!" She shouted angrily at the ceiling. She had absolutely no patience for anyone, and it felt good to release all the built-up tension. The noise was constant with no break and on top of it, the people were now blaring music. Her neighbor really decided to throw a party, now? She couldn't believe her day could get worse. She grabbed her grey zip and put it over her white tee shirt. She put her hair up in a high tail and slid into a pair of white high waisted jeans and the same white sneakers.

Once again, her sneakers hit the fuzzy grey carpet, and she walked out the door.

Chapter 2

As Addison began walking, she laid her eyes on the cold body who'd stained the grey carpet. There were three policemen each talking into their walkie-talkies reporting every bit of detail. She walked past the wall where the bullet still remained to the ground untouched. The wall above it chipped. She took a deep breath in and shook off the feeling that someone was watching her. She was steaming with anger. Walking so fast her tail was swaying side to side. She pressed the elevator button and looked up. The elevator was on the tenth floor. "Hurry!" Addison muttered under her breath while walking up and down.

She could still hear the booming music from the elevator. It made her even angrier. The elevator finally arrived, and she ran in and began pushing the button for the sixth floor continuously until she arrived at the sixth floor. She walked out without looking and walked straight into what felt like a wall.

She looked up to see a guy wearing a pair of dark blue jeans and a grey hoodie. His hood was up and left his face nothing but a mere shadow.

"Watch it!" The voice behind the hood said. His hair fell in front of his face and was the only thing visible. It was black and slightly curly. He brushed it back into the hood. "I'm so sorry, I wasn't looking where I was going. It's my fault.

"Addison quickly said, trying to get past the man.

"How about you open your eyes?" He said while pushing the button for the elevator that had now left.

Addison paid no attention to him and kept looking down the hallway where the noise was coming from.

"I don't remember seeing you around." She paused "You must be new, I'm Addison."

She turned around to see she was talking to a closed elevator door. She rolled her eyes and began to make her way down the hallway.

There it was number 78, the apartment directly above hers. She braced herself and knocked on the door twice. No reply, no voices, just music playing. She knocked again, louder this time. Once again silence. Fed up, she began pounding loudly on the door.

"Hello?! I know you are home I can hear your music from downstairs." She shouted.

She'd been so distracted with knocking on the door she hadn't noticed it was open. She looked down at the door's lock and saw it was broken.

As if someone had broken in. "Huh, that's weird." she thought to herself. She carefully pushed the door open and walked inside the apartment. It was almost identical to hers. The kitchen in the exact same place. The only difference was that this apartment was completely empty and deserted, with only a small radio plugged into a large speaker which was facing down onto the floor playing an oddly familiar song. Addison had a quick look around and decided that it must be some type of prank. She turns around to see the door had shut. Confused, she looks at the Handel and discovers a note.

~ *I never miss.*

October 12th, 8:30 pm, Lakewood park bench. Don't be late.

Addison dropped the note. Her eyes widened in fear as she realized the man in the hood sounded strangely familiar. Her heart was pounding. She scrambled out of the apartment and into the hallway. Her mind running all over the place, she began to get flashbacks.

First the fight with Alex. She played back every blow he threw at her. Then she curled up in a ball against the wall, her diving behind the wall and the bullet missing her by inches.

His voice saying "Hurt you? Love, I wouldn't dream of it." His deep British accent echoed in her head and it morphed into the voice of the man behind the hood.

"Watch it!" "How about you open your eyes."

The feeling she had a few hours ago returned. She was breathing but there was no air again.

Her heart beating even faster she stabbed wildly at the elevator button that was taking too long to arrive. She had no time. She wasn't safe. She ran down the stairs and into the safety of her apartment. Leaving all the police officers staring. She shut the door and used both locks to close it. She began hyperventilating as she took her sweatshirt off. She got light-headed. Everything was spinning. She reached in front of her but everything went black. Addison fell hitting her head on the hard-tiled ground.

Addison's vision blacked out for what felt like hours. She woke up on her floor. A nasty gash to her head left a throbbing headache. "Perfect. Just perfect this is exactly what I needed." She said with her hand on her head. Addison had a black eye and now a gash to her head. She stood up and looked out the window to see the sun was rising. The date was October 18th. Today was the day she was meant to meet the stranger who had shot a gun at her. Why was she even going?

She ran into her room and took a hot shower. She got dressed and headed out into her living room and looked at her reflection through the mirror. "You're strong. You're powerful. Most of all you're okay." She took a deep breath in and covered her bruise with foundation and makeup. She isn't the type of person who wears heavy makeup. She hates covering up her freckles.

When she was a little girl, her grandfather would always tell her that her freckles are the best part of her and that no one should ever tell her otherwise. She was very close to him. She would spend hours talking to him. When he died, she was twelve. The doctors said he died of a heart attack but deep inside her she knew he wasn't gone. That he would always be with her. He left her a locket with a picture of the both of them. That locket is one of her most prized possessions.

Her day at the office passed her in a flash, and she got back home. She put her key in her apartment door and opened it. She walked in and threw off her black high heels. She looked at her door and saw that there was a letter on the floor. She leaned down and picked up the letter. It was the same note from before. It had been folded many times and had some of the ink smudged and a ring of coffee on it. She took a deep breath in and looked at the clock. It was time. The sun had set a while back and it was pitch black outside. The only light came from the moon and the flickering street lights.

She changed into a pair of black high wasted jeans and a fluffy white sweater. She slid on her boots and went out the door. She walked down the street and into the park. There was a stone trail which she walked down for a few minutes. She took a deep breath in and could smell the rain left on the leaves. She found herself on a bench looking down at the beautiful lake in front of her. There was a dark oak tree that was turning yellow. She took a deep breath in and out. Soon enough she realized she was crazy. She had no idea why she had even come. He obviously wasn't going to show up and even if he did. This was obviously a trap.

Addison got up and looked around. She decided this was the wrong decision. She knew she should have gone to the police. He killed a man. He shot a bullet at her. Why did she think this was a good idea? All of a sudden, she heard a twig snap.

She began walking back up the pathway the way she came from but right before she could leave, she heard the same voice she'd heard that night. "What's the rush love?"

Her heart stopped. She gulped and turned around.

"What do you want from me?" she said nervously.

"Hello to you too." He said, smirking.

"You tried to shoot me; you could have killed me!" Addison said with a serious face. "I don't see how that's funny." She added after seeing him on the verge of bursting out laughing.

"I'm sorry you're right." He said and returned to his emotionless face. He then added on "It's not funny, it's bloody hilarious." He then burst out laughing and walked over to the bench and sat down.

Addison watched him like a hawk and said nothing. She studied him. His eyes were dead but somehow so young and innocent. That was until he returned to his serious face. He was a different man when he laughed.

"So, Addison Willmar, the one that got away." His voice was like an addicting poison that Addison could listen to for hours.

"How... How did you know my name?! Who are you?" Addison gasped.

"Who am I? Oh wow, you really are clueless." His laugh returned to his smirk.

"Who the hell are you and how do you know my name?" Addison demanded to know the truth. She'd had enough of this guy's mind games.

Addison moved closer to him and sat down on the bench. He looked her in the eye and for some reason Addison didn't feel scared any more. She felt no worry, she felt no pain. For those few seconds, Addison felt nothing. However, like all good things, it came to an end.

"My name's Adan Gibbson. I'm a trained hitman." His words echoed through the air and danced around her ears. His face became cold and stiff like a stone.

"A hitman?!" She shouted.

"Say it a bit louder, Mars didn't quite hear you." He said bitterly.

"Why are you here, with me? Are you after me?" she paused to think and before Adan had a chance to reply she added. "Oh, God...You're going to kill me. You're going to kill me here and bury me in the woods." She said quickly and began to feel uneasy...

"I'm going to die alone, cold and scared! Oh, my mother, my poor mother, she's going to be devastated. You can't... You can't kill me!" Addison shouted at him studying her surroundings for an escape.

"How about next time you don't meet the madman in the woods when it's pitch-black outside?" Adan said while keeping a straight face.

"Any last words?" Addison's face dropped, and she began looking around her for help...

Out of nowhere. The dark blue sky turned black and grey. The wind began blowing and the leaves danced around them. Adan moved closer to her and brushed her shining, silky, golden hair behind her ear. "It's a shame. I'm sorry love but..." He was cut off by the sudden buckets of water pouring from the sky. Once a storm like that starts, it never stops.

The cold rain fell from the sky so fast and hard they had no time to react. Addison's hair was all wet, she was soaked. Adan wore a leather jacket and a black button-up shirt. He had a pair of black ripped jeans on and black tie-up army boots. They both sat on a bench staring into each other's eyes. Addison looked terrified at Adan. He had no reaction, no emotion once again he was a statue. His dark grey eyes sparkled in the rain. Adan couldn't hold a straight face for much longer. He burst out laughing. "You should see your face right now."

He paused to catch his breath. "Oh god. I can't believe your face. It's hilarious." He added and continued laughing.

Addison looked so confused. She didn't know what just happened. Less than a few seconds ago she was discussing where she'd be buried. She tried to open her mouth to speak, but she froze. She was at a loss of words. Adan was laughing and for some inexplicable reason, at some point, Addison joined in. There they were. They looked like two normal people sitting on a bench in a park, having the time of their lives.

The rain was dripping off them, but they couldn't care less, they sat on that bench, drenched, laughing uncontrollably. They didn't need words. They didn't need time. They didn't need anything. Their bubble of joy was burst by a loud bolt of lightning hitting nearby followed by the loud crack of thunder. Addison shrieked and jumped up. She flung her arms around him and held on tight. For that brief moment, Adan felt something he'd never felt before. He felt warm, he felt at home in her arms, but he would die before he let anyone see that. He shook the feeling off.

"We should get inside." He said while standing up. "yeah you're right we should." Addison said while shivering. They walked together out the park and back to her apartment lobby.

"So, if you're not here to kill me, why are you here? And how did you know my name?" Addison said while staring into his majestic eyes. He was tall at least 6 ft 2. He towered over her. It should have made her feel afraid but instead, it made her feel safe and looked after.

"I was hired to look after you. I'm here to protect you." He said with a straight face. Addison's smile disappeared as she waited for him to laugh and silence fell across the room. Addison burst out laughing. "Ha, you actually got me," she said while waiting for Adan to say his part. To admit it's a joke. Adan didn't budge. He remained stiff and cold. "Addison, I'm not..." He tried to say but Addison interrupted him.

"Protect me?!" She shouted. "Protect me by shooting at me?!" She added on.

"Addison lower your voice." He snapped back, any trace of the Adan who held her in the rain had dissolved into the man standing in front of her. The man standing in front of her was a trained killer. Addison took a step back from him.

"I had fun Adan but I'm going home now." She said while backing away further.

"Addison, wait!" He took a deep breath in. "You need me here. You can't be alone anymore. The people who are after you, they don't mess around. They don't fail. You need to believe me and listen to me when I tell you that you aren't safe."

Addison looked him up and down and finally said "What is this? Some cheesy spy movie.

Adan no one is after me. No one knows me. I'm a loser. Trust me and believe me when I tell you no one is after…"

Addison was interrupted by Adan shouting. "Damn it, Addison, can you not be naive for a second and listen. There are teams of trained killers nearly as good as me who are coming after you. You really want to risk that?!"

Addison backed up all the way into the wall. Her hands by her side.

"Who? Who is after me?!" She shouted.

Chapter 3

Two men sat in chairs in front of the stainless-steel desk. They wore a formal uniform consisting of a blue blazer, matching dress pants, a black button-up shirt, Black polished shoes and a white tie. The man on the left had chestnut brown hair and whiskey-colored eyes. The man on the left seemed younger than him. He had glowing blond hair and sparkling blue eyes. In front of them, sat the man behind his desk. He sat in a grand office chair that had the impression of a throne. This man was feared. He sat looking at the wall which made the only thing visible to the men in the back of his chair.

"Boss, you asked for us?" the man with the whiskey man said in a shaky voice. The mysterious man remained silent behind his throne. The two men exchanged worried looks. "Maybe it was a mistake, and he didn't call us.

We should probably leave" the man with the blond hair whispered into his partner's ear. The two men quietly got up from their chairs and began tiptoeing towards the big, dark cherry wood double doors. As they placed their hands on the handle, all hell broke loose and the man behind the throne finally spoke.

"Sit down you fools!" He shouted. The room remained silent as his voice diffused into the past. His actions reminded them of how dangerous he could be.

The men knew better than to talk. You see, they've been working for this man for the past 5 years. The last man to question his actions had his fingers one by one delivered to the front porch of his family via second class. This man, the man in his throne was no ordinary man. He was a man most men feared, a man who haunted the dreams of men. He was a Maniac who felt no emotions. The silence seemed to drag on for ages. He finally spoke.

"I've summoned you because the earth has shifted on its axes, and we have lost eyes on our target." His voice was bitter and chilly.

One of the men looked up at the screen above the boss's chair and began to read.

"Target name: Addison Willmar. Target Age: 26. Target location: unknown."

Both the men looked at each other and the one with the blond hair said, "Location unknown? There must be some type of error." "Whoever updated the chart must be wrong." The other man exclaimed.

The man behind the chair chuckled and paused for a moment. The two men imminently knew they had messed up. "I updated the chart you fool! There is no mistake. Our target has gone under the radar, and we can't seem to find her." His voice made the men shake in their chairs.

The man took a deep breath in and continued. "This brings me to the reason I summoned you. I have a plan and some new intel."

The man behind the chair took a deep breath and began to speak again. "We know she couldn't have gone far. She doesn't know anything is going on. She's clueless"

"How are we going to find her?" The man with the whisky hair said.

The man behind the chair spun around throwing a knife at the man's head missing by millimeters, the knife burying itself the wall behind him. "I am the one who asks the questions here." The man had bright blue eyes and dark brown hair parted to one side. One of his eyes had a yellowish, purple circle of bruising around it. He looked infuriated. "How we're going to find her doesn't matter. The only thing that does is that she will pay for everything he has done. She will pay with the life of everyone she loves and her own." He shouted across the desk into their faces. The grand double doors swung open suddenly and a young woman walked in. She had dark brown hair and grey eyes.

"Alex you have a call." She said while holding a phone in her hand.

Addison had taken the past few days off work. In the period of those few days, her life had been tipped onto its head. With everything else going on she couldn't deal with her boss as well. Two nights ago, she met up with the man she had witnessed commit murder and found out that his job was to protect her from dangerous people. Addison stood in front of her bathroom mirror.

"Okay, so it's been a really weird week." She said looking at her neatly gelled back hair tied up into a sleek bun. She then looked at her bruised eye that she had tried to cover up. The foundation wouldn't cover anything, it was turning yellow. She glanced at her watch. 7:40 AM. She was meant to walk out the door ten minutes ago.

She scanned the room and laid her eyes on a pair of sunglasses. She placed them on her face.

"You're just going to have to do it, I'm out of time." She said as she walked to her door and put on her black high heel shoes. She wore a black pencil skirt that reached just above her knees, a white blouse and a light blue blazer. She took a deep breath as she opened her door and muttered under her breath,

"Here we go again. Hopefully this time no murderer." She smiled at her own joke and took the elevator down to the ground floor. She pushed the glass door and she was now outside. It was a chilly October morning and the wind was blowing.

She looked around and began walking down her street when all of a sudden, her phone began ringing inside her bag. She reached in and saw her screen light up with her mother's name. She slid her finger across her phone and placed it to her ear, "Hi, mom." she said and began catching up with her mother. However, when it came to telling her mother about Alex and the murder, she had just spent time with, she kept her

43

mouth shut. She'd been so distracted she wasn't looking where she was going and walked straight into someone. Her phone was knocked out of her hand and hit the ground. "Oh my god, I'm so sorry!" She quickly picked her phone up and told her mom she'd call her back soon. After hanging up she finally looked up.

"Adan?" She asked while looking up at those familiar grey eyes she'd lost herself in not too long ago.

Adan wore black jeans, sneakers and a leather jacket. "We need to stop meeting like this." He said and let out a chuckle.

"What are you doing here?" Addison said while looking around her.

"Following you. I told you I'm here to protect you." His smile began to fade.

"And I told you I don't need your protection. No one is after me. I'm not in danger."

"I'm afraid it's not that easy. They're going to come for you eventually. Better safe than sorry right?" His classic smile returned.

"You're stalking me and you've managed to make me late for work." Her tone was cold, and she was beginning to get annoyed.

"Now if you don't mind please get out my way." She said while putting her phone in her bag.

"Addison..." He began and put his hand on her shoulder. He looked her in the eye and continued. "You have no reason to trust or believe me, I get that, but all I ask of you is to go back home. Don't come out. You're not safe."

Addison remained silent for a while and then shook off his hand. "Get out of my way Adan. We wouldn't want me to cause a scene now, would we?" She said while walking past him. She continued walking into her office building and didn't look back once.

The day at work flew by and it quickly passed. Walking back home, she analyzed everyone. Something inside her knew that Adan may just be telling the truth. She ran into her apartment building and quickly made her way back into her apartment. She took her shoes off and walked into her bedroom, got changed into pyjamas and walked into her kitchen. She opened her fridge and took out some vegetables. She grabbed a chopping board and placed it onto the counter and heard a crunch. Confused, she lifted the board to reveal her locket.

The same locket her grandfather had given her was broken into a million little pieces.

"What the..." she said puzzled while running her fingers over her neck to check. She didn't remember taking it off. She never took it off. Her grandfather gave her the locket a couple of months before he died suddenly. She was twelve when he gave it to her, and she'd had it for fourteen years and not once had she taken it off.

How on earth did it make its way onto the counter smashed into a million pieces?

Addison held onto the counter until the whole world stopped spinning. She didn't know what to feel. She was angry, sad, puzzled but most of all betrayed. Whoever did this obviously knew that locket meant the world to her. She felt frozen on the spot. She picked up the locket's pieces that were so small they'd be mistaken for dust and sunk to the floor. Her eyes overflowed with tears, and she began to sob uncontrollably. There was one thing in this whole world she had left of her grandfather, one thing in this world she valued more than anything and now it was dust. It was broken into a puzzle with thousands of missing parts.

Addison sat there on the floor when all of a sudden three sharp knocks radiated throughout the whole apartment and caused her to jump. She got up and scooped the locket pieces into a little box and walked over to the door. She wiped her tears and opened the door to reveal a face she never thought she'd see again.

"What the hell do you want?!" She shouted at him. Alex stood straight wearing all black. A color he refused to wear before. His face was straight, and he said, "I'm so sorry Addison. I never wanted to hurt you." He paused and moved his hand over to Addison's eye making her wince in pain.

She slapped his arm away and bitterly said, "A bit too late for that."

"Come on, you know I love you so much, I can't live without you. I refuse to live without you." He blurted out.

"Alex, get the hell out of my face. You and your pathetic excuses are the last things I want to deal with right now." She remained calm and tried to close the door only to see that Alex's foot was in the way. "Addison, I love you! Please just let me in and we can figure something out!" He tried his luck once again, trying to push the door open.

"Get out of my door now or I will break your foot off. You really don't want to test me, not after the week I've just had." Her voice had changed; it wasn't sweet. Her voice was dead, she had nothing to lose any more.

"Addison, I don't know what happened to you but you aren't the same person I've known for the last three years." Addison let go of the door and stopped trying to close it. "You want to come in?" She asked and Alex nodded. "You want to talk?" She asked and once again he nodded.

Addison stood with her hands on the door. The door was wide open and Alex stood confused studying Addison. "So, can I come in now?" He asked.

"Yeah sure come in!" Addison said smiling and as Alex was about to walk in, she slammed the door hard into his head. "Come into this house and I promise you, you won't come out again!"

Addison shouted through her door. From then on there was silence. Addison returned to the kitchen and carried the box to her couch. She placed it down on her side table and the next thing she knew. She'd fallen asleep.

Chapter 4

The next thing Addison heard was a scream which awoke her from her sleep. She jumped up and onto her feet.

Confused, she looked at the clock which showed 19:52. "It must have been my imagination..." Addison was interrupted by another scream, louder this time and full of pain and fear. Adrenaline flushing her veins she rushed to her door and unlocked it. She looked around for a weapon and grabbed an umbrella. Hugging her weapon, she opened her door and stuck her head out of her door to see nothing but an empty hallway. The scream came back, it sounded closer this time. She ran out of her house leaving the door open. "Hello?" She said, not knowing what to expect as a reply. She heard loud, heavy footsteps approaching her and turned around.

"Alex, for God's sake! I told you to leave" She shouted while sighing in relief.

"Come with me," Alex said.

"As if, keep dreaming!" Addison replied to him.

"Oh..." Alex began to laugh. "She thought I was asking." "Who are you talking to?" puzzled Addison turned around and saw two men behind her and added. "What the hell is this Alex?" she said dropping her umbrella onto the floor...

"Let's call it repaying the favor," Alex said signaling to the men who then covered Addison's mouth and pulled a sack over her head.

Addison sat in the back of an old pick-up truck. Its paint was rusting orange. She sat in the back seat while Alex sat in the front seat. As soon as they put her in the car, she took off the dark, stuffy sack. The car was locked from the inside. Addison sat with her belt on looking out the window. "Alex?" She tried asking again. For the past two hours, he'd been ignoring her. He turned the radio up so that her voice would be hidden by the noise. All of a sudden, the car came to a sudden stop and the seat belt cut into Addison's neck. "Watch it!" Addison yelled in pain. Alex finally turned back and looked at her. "You made this hard," he said while staring into her eyes. He'd waited for this moment for so long, yet some part of him still refused to agree with the plan for the woman he'd fallen in love with. Some small part of him was still human. Some small part of him knew this was all wrong. "You know, some part of me wants to let you go, to let you live." Alex said while keeping his stiff, cold face emotionless. "So, let me go! It's not too late." She attempted to convince him but Alex was too smart, too diabolical.

He clicked his seatbelt off and stepped out of the car. Addison sat in that car as if she was an animal in a cage, being poked and laughed at. She was burning with anger. She wasn't afraid. She knew she had to get out of it. Alex, as smart as he was, had one weakness. He couldn't stand her face because it brought back and all the good memories of the times, he'd had with her.

53

He stood outside the car rethinking his plan. He finally walked around the car to Addison's door. He opened it and helped her out the car. "I see you've come to your senses" Addison's voice enraged him and pushed him over the edge. The next thing Addison saw was the inside of a dark abandoned room. She lifted her head and tried to move her hands to brush her hair out of her eyes only to see that her hands were tied behind her back to some type of column. She began taking deep breaths in. This wasn't how the plan had unfolded in head.

Alex was meant to have let her go. But now she was sitting on a cold floor. Her eyes slowly adjusted to the darkness, and she began looking around her. She saw a large floor to ceiling window which was shattered to her left. Outside the window, she could see the long grass swaying and the stars in the dark night sky. She looked around the inside of the room. It was a large room; she could only see a bit of it. The floors were dark black tiles and the walls were made of dark red brick. The rest of this room was pitch black.

With her heart in her throat, she quickly saw that she was in danger. Her instincts kicked in, and she began screaming, making the remaining glass still attached to the walls vibrate.

"Help! Help me! Anyone, please help!" She screamed as loud as her lungs would let her. She drained every bit of energy she had and realized it was no help. No one could hear. Her last scream fell to the ground like snow and dissipated.

Out of the corner of the darkness a voice said, "Oh no, please do continue the show." and then began laughing.

"This is funny?!" Addison demanded to know who the face behind the voice was.

Alex stepped out of the darkness. "Of course, it is, you should see your face."

"Alex!" Addison started shouting but couldn't continue, her voice was too tired.

"Let me go." She said while struggling for air.

"Let me go!" she demanded once again.

"Where would the fun in that be?" He chuckled once more and began walking toward her. The sound of his shoes hitting the ground with every step he took was nearly louder than the screaming voices in her head. She looked up from the ground, still struggling to breathe.

"You're so petty." She said while letting a small smile onto her face and shaking her head.

"You have such a pathetic life; your ego is so sensitive and fragile you can't accept that no one will ever want you." She stopped to catch her breath.

Alex's face began turning pale and her words hit him like flying daggers sinking into his skin. "Careful there." He said, dripping in anger.

"What's wrong? Don't like the truth, no one ever does. I didn't love you. Dearest mommy sure as hell couldn't stand you." she was interrupted by Alex shouting "Shut up! Just close your mouth before you say something you will surely regret."

"Something I'll regret?" Addison said while raising an eyebrow. "Oh, I know." She burst out laughing and then added: "Should I not mention your father then?"

Addison felt a sharp stinging pain on her face followed by the wet feeling of blood dripping from her nose. Her vision began to cloud and she blacked out completely. Her head hitting the cold ground with a thud she couldn't hear.

Alex continued punching her even after she passed out. He got up and gathered himself. He walked back into the darkness and came back dragging a large device with him. He set the timer to thirty minutes and pressed the set button. He then began walking out. He stepped outside and took a deep breath in. He calmed himself and sank to the ground. "Damn it!" He banged his hands on the muddy grass until his hands were black and purple.

"If only I could have stopped him. I'm sorry dad. I'm so sorry I couldn't help you." he shouted at the sky and drew his attention back to the warehouse where Addison was.

"I hope this is enough for you to forgive me. I know it won't bring you back, at least you can rest in peace." He got up dusted off his pants and walked off into the sunset.

Chapter 5

This part is written in Addison's point of view.

Addison:

I stood in the middle of this warehouse, it was abandoned and there was an occasional breeze. A big shattered window and broken bricks all over. The place was crawling with spiders. I looked around and I felt no pain. I felt no fear. I felt nothing. The more I thought about it the more I remembered. Until the moment it all came back. All those memories of the past twenty-four hours flooded my mind. Everything returned. That feeling that was so heavy I couldn't move. The type of feeling that makes you want to throw up. I pushed it aside, I buried it which only made it worse, but I knew I couldn't waste any time.

I walked around the warehouse and discovered a girl. Her honey yellow hair was tied back, with bits of it in her eyes. She wore black sweatpants and a grey tee shirt. Every step I took closer to her I felt some type of resistance as if something was pushing me back. The closer I got the more my face hurt, until I finally reached her. I kneeled down and untied her hands from behind her. I brushed the hair out of her eyes. She was unconscious. When I tried to touch her to wake her up, that throbbing pain disappeared. I felt relieved. I shook her but she wouldn't wake up. I looked around to see if there was something that could help me with her. I discovered right next to us, a timer, counting down. It had about fifteen minutes left on it.

The silence screamed into my ears. I heard drops, hitting the ground. I looked out the window but the sky was clear there was no rain. Confused, I looked at the ground and saw a pool of blood on the floor under her face. Her nose had been bleeding. When I went to touch her to lift her head off the cold ground, my nose also started bleeding and the throbbing unbearable pain returned in my head. I realized that the injured, unconscious girl I was observing on the floor, was really me. "Addison, wake up!" I needed to wake up. Time was running faster and faster. Whatever happens at the end of that timer was surely not going to be very pleasant. This rush of adrenaline overtook me like a spell, as if a switch had suddenly been flipped. I felt my insides turning inside out. I needed to get us both out of here.

I grabbed her arms and began dragging her towards the exit, I had no idea how to find. "Addison!" I kept screaming my own name, each time I. could feel the pain getting more powerful, I couldn't anymore. I'd reached a limit. I slumped down on the floor and laid my head on the ground. Blackness overcame me quickly. I was awoken by the continuous laughter of a child. I opened my eyes and felt the hard, scratchy grass against my face. I stood up pulling grass out of my hair. "Higher grandpa. Higher!" a very familiar voice began saying while laughing. It sounded like the voice of a little girl. Her voice was sweet, pure and innocent. I followed the high-pitched laughter that could break a grass and I saw a man I never thought I would see again.

In front of me was a little girl on a plastic swing attached to a large cherry oak tree. She had the lightest, bright blue eyes ever. Her hair was silky and freely dancing around her face as the swing she rode went up and down. Her smile was pure and worth millions. Behind he was an older man, in his late fifties.

He had the same blue eyes as the little girl, his hair was gelled down but still curly. His presence brought tears to my eyes.

"Grandpa!" I shouted as I ran towards him. He didn't seem to hear, so I shouted again "Grandpa?!" I ran in front of the swing as it was in the air.

I looked him in the eye and for a split-second, I felt like he saw me, I felt like I did before he died.

"Grandpa it's me." Before he could say anything, I felt a sharp stabbing pain in my stomach and fell to the ground.

A loud explosion echoed and dissipated into the air. I felt the gentle warmth on my face. Once again, my vision blurred out...blackness again. It seemed like hours turned into years. The blackness once again faded out and I stood up. A white haze hung around the whole place, like a sunny gaze on an early summer morning. My head was pounding with pain.

I once again set eyes on my grandfather. This time was different. He was different. Not in a good way. His clothes were shredded and broken. His skin has patches of dirt on them. He was almost unrecognizable. He looked just as confused, out of place and terrified as me. That was true until he set eyes on me. It was as if all his pain was erased. His frown erased itself and his smile awoke. "Is... Is that really you?" His voice was trembling with happiness.

"Yeah, yes, it's really me grandpa, is that really you?" I said letting my eyes cloud with tears of overwhelming happiness. We stood 6 feet apart. He ran up to me and hugged me. I felt his warmth when all of a sudden, all the clouds in the sky split.

"You're not meant to be here. Not yet." He said, his smile slowly dropping.

"Addison you need to listen now, no talking just listening. You are going to climb that staircase and you are never going to look back. You will never think of this again because I promise you that you will always be okay. They will never be a reason for you to be scared as long as I'm here. I love you, Adi. It's time for you to go back home." The sun slid behind the clouds and turned black.

"GO!" he shouted loudly.

"No! I've just found you again." I didn't want to leave. I never wanted to leave but for some reason, my body knew I needed to leave. This wasn't a place I was welcome in. I looked up at the sky tearing in two. A bright blinding light let a staircase fall out of it. I ran up the silky marble stairs getting dizzier as I did. That world was so far behind it felt like a dream. My eyes opened. Reality sunk in. I could see everything yet I felt so blind. It wasn't blurry but it was hazy. I thought I forgot it all. I thought it was a dream. I hoped it was all a dream but as reality sunk in, the truth came back and all I could do was weep...

My eyes were open. I was breathing. Reality began to sink back in. Just as my vision returned, I felt a sharp pain in my stomach and memories began to return. Each memory was more painful than the other.

I began to remember the man I spent three years with, had kidnapped me. The fury began to flush through my skin. I lifted my head off the ground and looked around registering every small detail. The sky was full of colors. There was pink, red, orange and blue in the sky. It was breathtaking. Not too far away there was a wall of tall leafless trees. Before the wall of trees, there was a field of yellow grass. I drew my attention to the rubble I was sitting in. Directly in front of me, was the heavy stone foundation of the warehouse. I was surrounded by sharp, crystal shards of glass and old crumbling brick.

I began replaying the previous hours in my head and I could remember everything, almost everything. Alex had tied me up in that warehouse, the warehouse that was standing right in front of me last time I'd opened my eyes. I'd said some things to Alex, which drove him over the edge.

I had expertly added salt to the wound. He knocked me out and that's when I saw grandad. I must have been hallucinating. I lifted my arm to my face and flinched as I touched my swollen eye. The pain flashed through me. When I drew my hand away from my face, it was full of blood. Aside from my face and my stomach and the pain, I wasn't too badly damaged. I put my hands on the ground in front of me and made it back up onto my feet. That's when it hit me. That's when it all came back. My memories came rushing back like water from a broken dam.

Aden came in. He untied my hands and lifted me up. He walked out just in time. Seconds after he carried me out, the warehouse blew like an angry volcano. I couldn't help but smile, he'd been watching me this whole time. He was like a guardian angel. That's if you could ignore the whole hitman side of him. I began looking around with my smile reaching my eyes. He'd really saved me. He'd been right this whole time. All I could see was rubble. Big pieces of bricks and broken glass all over.

My smile slowly dropped and time froze as it hit me. Adan was nowhere to be seen.

"No, no, no, no," I screamed under my breath.

The panic in my eyes began to blur my vision. "Adan!" My voice echoed for miles, but he was still nowhere to be seen.

"Adan!" I rushed over to a big piece of concrete and struggled to lift it up. "He saved me. He doesn't get to die!" I began screaming at the sky. "He saved me! Don't you dare take him!" The anger gave me strength and I finally managed to flip the concrete over. It weighed more than a car to me.

My heart beat heavily from the effort. I don't know what I expected to find under it. Disappointment and fear suddenly drowned me. I was trapped in my own prison of feelings. I spent the rest of the time until sunset, flipping and lifting pieces of concrete and screaming helplessly at the sky as if it would bring him back.

When the light failed, I worked frantically to the faint light of the moon scratching away at the rubble.

I was hungry, I was thirsty, I was tired but there was no way I was going to stop searching. My heart seemed to hurt physically from my anguish. My whole body was in agony. I was alone with only the moon to hear my cries.

I slumped down on the floor, my clothes filthy and dripping in sweat and my face bruised and throbbing in pain. All I wanted to do was go back. I wanted to go back to him, to my grandfather. I wanted to relive those moments with him for the next century. I needed to escape. The thoughts of him, made me smile just for a second. I was convinced Adan was already too far gone to save, but I wasn't stopping until I found him, I owed him at least that. I forced myself to get back up.

The clouds up in the sky had covered the moon and all I could see now were shapes and figures. The wind began howling. I wasn't the least scared. I was driven by my motivation to find him. I began walking in the one direction I'd tried to avoid this whole time. The warehouse itself. I was so tired and cold that I had to drag myself there. My shoe caught under a rock and just like that I was face down in the rubble, with a mouth full of dust.

"Why?!" I spat in frustration.

I couldn't bother trying to get back up. I lay on the ground and listened to the noises of the night. There was an owl not too far away, something howling and the sound of crickets in the night. It calmed me down and made me feel not so alone. Even though the cold had started nibbling at me, I stayed on the ground and slowly came to terms that at some point I would have to stop looking and try to save myself. I hated that it had come to this point.

I relaxed my whole body and closed my eyes. I don't know how long I'd drifted off for, but I woke up to the sound I'd convinced myself I'd never hear again. "Giving up so fast love?" His voice was unbothered and effortless. At that moment my soul left my body. I lifted myself onto my feet struggling, pushing the pain aside and burst out laughing at the sight of his face.

He was wearing his signature white button-up shirt and black jeans with business shoes. His shirt was ripped and muddy. His face was full of little cuts. I stared in amazement and he did the same back. I took a deep breath in. My face hurt from smiling so much, but there was no way I would stop smiling. I ran over to him but before I could reach him. He sank onto his knees, collapsed onto the rubble filled ground with a sickening thud and passed out. I froze on the spot and swallowed hard.

Chapter 6

Addison fought every bit of fear in her and continued walking towards the lifeless body of Adan. She knew better than to cry. He was lying on the ground so peacefully, as if he was sleeping.

She kneeled down next to him and gently lifted his head to hold it. She'd managed to push all her roaring feelings aside and somehow turned her survival mode on. Her shaking hand made its ways onto Adan's neck. She pressed two fingers against his soft warm skin to feel for a pulse. She held it there for a few seconds, and she eventually felt a rhythm.

The relief on her face was strong and fierce. She cradled his head and began to think again. She knew she had to get him to a hospital. She kept one hand on his neck, continually checking his pulse.

"Adan, I need you to wake up. please." Her voice was sweet and low, almost as if she was whispering. She took a deep breath in fighting back the tears and added.

"Please."

Adan slowly opened his eyes. He was clearly struggling to breathe but managed to get a few words in.

"I'm hurt." He said without panicking.

"You don't say." Addison had a trace of a smile that faded with her voice.

Adan took another breath in gathering his thoughts and added

"My car is a few miles South. You're going to find my phone in there." He paused to catch his breath.

His lips were dry and his face was bloody. "Call Nico and tell him I'm calling in my favor. Turn on the GPS and stay in the car until he gets here." He took another deep breath in.

"You're also coming. I don't need to know what to do because you're going to be there." Addison painted a sympathetic smile onto her face while brushing his hair out of his eyes.

"Addison. Go!" He commanded without hesitation. "I'm not leaving." Addison was stern and stubborn.

"Then we're both going to die out here together because of your stubbornness. Go!" He tried to use anger to mask his pain.

Addison fought every instinct in her body and gently positioned his head on the soft grass nearby. She got up and walked away staring back at him. She said nothing to him because she knew she would get another chance to. She walked calmly into the darkness until she reached a point where he couldn't see her any more, and she started to run. She ran as she had never done before. She ran like her life depended on it. She was surrounded by long grass, in a field. Half an hour later, she stumbled on to a road. It was still pretty hidden from civilization but it gave her some hope.

She saw a black SUV parked on the shoulder. Instinct told her that was his car, and she knew she was right when she peered into the window and saw his phone between the front seats.

She tried the door. It was locked, looked around and saw a long sharp, heavy rock in the long grass. She bent down and with all her pent-up anger and fear she closed her eyes, and she hurled it through the closed window. She reached her shaky hand into the car to get to the unlock button between the seats. She pushed the button and the doors unlocked. As she pulled her arm back through the shattered window, a piece of sharp glass sliced through the fragile skin of her right hand. She winced in pain, pulled back her arm quickly and took a deep breath in.

She opened the car door, brushed away some of the glass and sat down in the driver's seat. Blood began dripping down her right hand. She leaned over and used her left hand to open the passenger's glove compartment. Inside she found a bright green first aid kit. She took it out and placed it on the passenger seat. There was a phone, a notepad and some pens, a black and a white t-shirt and in the very back there was a gun. She wasn't surprised.

She took the phone into her left hand, leaving bloody fingerprints all over the car. She unlocked the phone and went to contacts, she searched 'Nico' and pressed the call button next to his name. The phone rang, each ring raising her heartbeat. It rang three times and halfway through the fourth a deep, robot-like voice answered. "It's 4 am, man." He sounded as if he'd just woken up. Addison hesitated to speak but finally said, "Um... Hello, my name is Addison and I, we need help." A long wait of silence followed. The man still said nothing. You could hear him breathing through the phone and waiting. After checking if he was still on the line Addison added, "Adan followed me after I was kidnapped and saved me, but he's," Addison

76

fought back tears. Raising her voice, she said, "He's hurt. He's badly hurt. He's calling in his favor."

The man let Addison's words fade before he said. "GPS" and hung up.

She imminently turned on the GPS on the phone. The dial tone remained in her head as she opened the first aid kit with her left hand.

She found a bandage and some gauze along with other plasters and medical equipment. She wrapped her hand with gauze watching the blood dye it red and added a tight bandage onto. She sat in the car for what felt like hours but in reality, was only twenty minutes.

She was staring out at the open road when she got an idea. She reached into the glove compartment and pulled out the gun. She took the first aid kit in her hand and got out of the car. As she was about to walk back down the field to Adan, she heard a car pull up. She dropped the first aid kit and tightened her grip on the gun. The car pulled up next to Adan's and a tall, muscular man with tattoos covering his arms and neck walked out. He wore denim jeans and a plain t-shirt.

"Where is he?" Addison immediately recognized his voice and let out a sigh of relief. "This way." She said, signaling for him to go first, she was still unsure of this Nico person.

They walked half the way in silence. Neither dared to ask questions. All of a sudden Nico stopped and Addison walked into him.

"Why the gun?" He asked.

"Keep walking." She said while ignoring him.

She then stopped and added, "It's my warranty." she smiled at him and walked up in front of him. Nico began laughing and followed her. A few minutes later, they arrived at the warehouse. Addison said nothing to Nico and began running towards Adan. He hadn't moved much. He was awake, but he wasn't moving, he lay there still, as if someone somewhere had pressed pause on a remote.

"Adan I'm here." She said, kneeling and looking up at Nico who was on the verge of laughter. Adan looked at Nico and Nico looked at Adan as if Addison didn't exist.

"Well don't just stand there. Help him!" Addison yelled at Nico. He burst out laughing and walked over to Adan. Addison and Nico had managed to get Adan back on his feet and get back to Nico's car. The whole ride there, she sat in the back seat with Adan's head on her lap watching the passing streets.

They drove through a crowded city and turned onto the almost empty highway. After a few hours, they turned off. The roads had no pavement and were surrounded by trees and bushes. Nico drove them over to Adan's house and helped them get inside. His house was a big five-bedroom Victorian house with a modern remodeled inside. Addison helped him to the couch and made Adan some tea. She cleaned all his wounds and found some painkillers to give him. They didn't do much talking.

"Pick any room and go get some rest." He told Addison who had been falling asleep on her feet. She nodded at him and walked off. His house was a maze compared to her tiny one-bedroom apartment. She walked into the first room she found and crashed onto the bed.

She'd never fallen asleep faster. In her sleep, her mind replayed the day over and over. Until eventually all she could see was black darkness. It slowly began to brighten up and her grandfather walked out of the shadows. She tried to speak. she fought to speak but she couldn't. She was only meant to listen. He walked over to her and hugged her. He calmed her down and wiped her tears, until eventually silence was broken, and he said,

"It's not over." Her grandfather began coughing and fell at her feet. She kneeled down in panic trying to help him, but she was unable to speak. She was screaming internally. He began coughing violently and blood began flowing out of the corners of his mouth.

"I'm sorry sweetheart. I'm sorry I've left my mess for you to clean up. I'm sorry."

Unable to scream or reply Addison began shaking him. She woke up screaming, back in the room she'd fallen asleep in. Adan ran into her room so fast; the door slammed open, door handle almost making a hole in the wall. She was panting and struggling to get air. Adan moved over to her and sat on the bed beside her. "It's okay. It was only a dream" He tried to reassure her. She knew it wasn't. She knew, he came to warn her.

Ever since that night that Addison woke up screaming, she knew her life would never be the way it was before.

She spent her week inside Adan's mansion. It was huge. There were cherry dark oak wood planks in all the common areas and hallways. Inside the bedrooms, there was a creamy soft beige carpet. The ceilings were tall and there was a yard outside the size of a supermarket parking lot. There were many pretty flowers and lots of open green space. He had a big swimming pool with a hot tub right by it. Addison knew exactly where his money came from but her mind couldn't help but wonder.

Adan knew that Alex wouldn't give up. The second he found out she was still alive; he'd do everything in his power to get his revenge and finish the job. He worried about it every hour. When he'd call her name, and she didn't respond, his mind would always wonder to the worst possibility.

Chapter 7

Adan healed more every day and he got better. Addison however, was physically healthy but her personality had changed. She had become cold. It was like she was dead inside.

A week after the incident, Addison had settled into the house. Adan had sent one of his friends to her apartment to fetch her things. In a matter of hours, everything of Addison's was packed in separate, neatly labelled, cardboard boxes. It had brought normality to her strange life. She'd taken over the largest room in the house, had spread out and had claimed it as her own. The room alone was the size of her whole apartment. There was a sitting area with two red velvet couches and a heavy brass coffee table.

It sat in front of a traditional stone fireplace. She loved to just sit in front of it on the furry carpet with a cup of hot cocoa and watch the flames slowly die down. Adan's room was one of the smallest rooms. He hated being alone in such a large house, he'd told her on the first day. But this house was off the grid and hidden, meaning no one would find her here. Addison sat up on her bed, pushing the silky blanket off her legs. She stretched her hands up towards the ceiling and yawned.

Her hair was all messed up. She wore a pair of white shorts and an oversized t-shirt that read "I'm not bossy. I'm the boss." She put her bare feet on the white warm carpet expecting to feel a cold stone floor but instead feeling the warmth of the carpet. She smiled and ran her hands through her hair trying to undo the knots in her hair on the way to her en-suite bathroom. She walked past the fireplace and folded up the blanket she'd left on the floor the evening before and placed it neatly on the back of the couch.

She yawned again and opened the white door with the golden handle to her bathroom. She stepped onto the marble flooring and received the cold shock she'd been expecting earlier. The cold travelled up her spine and seemed to wake her up. She walked over to the generous double sink and turned on the tap. She stared at herself in the mirror and smiled. She splashed some cold water onto her face and then brushed her teeth and washed her face. She jumped into her shower and had a hot relaxing shower. When she got out, she returned to her sink.

After looking at the white mirror frame, she discovered the corner of a photo behind it. After gently tugging on the photo she managed to get it out. It was a low-quality picture with a man wearing a suit who had blond hair and a young boy by him smiling.

She continuously stared at the picture until she realized the man with the blond hair was her grandfather. She walked over to her bed and placed the picture into the drawer beside her bed. She'd figured she'd ask about it later but curiosity roared in her head. Walking back into the bathroom, she picked up her hairbrush and brushed her hair. It wasn't a sun kissed blond any more. Her hair was an ashy brown. The water drops fell onto her shoulders in a rhythm. She put on some peachy eye shadow, Some brown mascara and a clear lip balm. She put her wet hair into a tight high ponytail and walked back into her room.

She opened her ashy built-in closet and brushed through the hangers until she picked out a pair of black yoga pants. A big baby blue knitted sweater. Some walked over to her wardrobe and found a pair of white and blue fuzzy socks which she put on over her yoga pants. She walked out of her room and down the grand double stairs. The grand clock in the hallway downstairs showed 07:32 am. She walked over into the kitchen where she saw Adan. "Morning." He said while holding his coffee in his and staring out of the big double doors leading to the garden. He wore a pair of black sweat pants and a tight white t-shirt. He took a sip of his coffee and looked at Addison grinning.

"Good morning Adan." She said laughing

She reached into the counter behind him and took out two plates. "Eggs?" She asked while turning on the stove and placing down a pan. Adan smiled and walked over to the fridge and got the ingredients for two fried eggs and placed them on the counter next to her. As she was cracking an egg he said, "You know we're training today right?"

"How could I forget?" She asked sarcastically, almost rolling her eyes.

She wasn't happy she had to train, but she did know it would help her, so she agreed. She slid the first egg on a plate and moved on to the second egg. They both sat down at the island near the counter and ate their eggs, talking about the different moves Adan would teach her. Adan took their dishes to the sink and walked Addison to the gym.

"Okay, go warm-up and then show me what you've got" Adan was excited to teach her.

Addison warmed up and then entered the boxing ring where Adan was punching the air. She took off her sweater to reveal a white tank top. They both began jumping on the spot. Adan threw a slow punch at her, and she ducked it.

She came back up and almost got Adan in the face, but he caught her punch. They went back and forth for hours until finally, Addison punched Adan across the face. She instantly regretted it and pulled her arm back but it was too late. Adan cracked his jaw and said "Good one."

"Well, what now?" Addison seemed tired and almost impatient. Adan ran up behind her and grabbed her, keeping her hands against her chest. "Never lose focus." He said Addison tried to fight her way out but gave up. He began laughing but as soon as he did, she managed to flip him over her head into the ground in front of her. She kneeled beside him and held his hand behind his back.

"Could say the same for you." She began laughing and released him. A few more hours passed, and they finished up for the day. They went into the kitchen and began talking about dinner. Addison took out a pot and as she went to get the pasta, she saw Adan had taken over. He loved cooking. The last thing anyone would expect was a tough guy like him cooking. Addison knew better than to argue. Instead, she poured both of them a glass of wine, and they spoke as the pasta boiled. They both sat down at the dining room table across from each other eating the pasta he'd made. "I still can't believe you pulled a guy on Nico," Adan said while laughing so hard he almost fell off his chair.

"Well, how was I supposed to know?!" Addison said, smiling. She looked at Adan, and they kept eye contact for a while until her smile dropped, and she turned her head and stared into space. "Addison?" Adam's accent made her name sound so much more exciting. She didn't respond. She was just staring at the lit fireplace.

"I'm sorry." He said, looking at her concerned.

"For? It's not your fault. It's mine. I did something to get Alex like that." she said looking up at him and down at her plate.

Adan stood up from his chair and didn't even tuck it in, he walked around the table to Addison and kneeled down by her chair.

"Don't you ever dare say it's your fault. It isn't that you haven't done anything. It wasn't you." He seemed upset she'd ever said that it was her fault. His face was full of compassion which she'd never seen before. She looked at him, and he brushed the hair out of her eyes and lifted up her chin.

"Then whose fault is it? Why is he after me?" She said while staring him in the eye.

"That's not my story to tell." Silence followed and all Adan did was stare her in the eyes. He loved her blue eyes. He leaned in closer to her making her lose her breath and kissed her. She was speechless, but she looked at him and questioned his actions waiting for him to say something.

"It doesn't matter." He said and paused. He looked at her and kissed her again. She kissed him back and the world stopped spinning. All her worry and problems faded away. "It's me and you against the world." His words echoed out through the night into every corner of existence. His words were true. It was them against the world.

Chapter 8

After that evening, time rushed as if it was stuck on fast-forward.

Day from day, Addison would wake up, get ready and spend the day training with him. Training for a moment she hoped would never arrive. She used to be a believer. She used to be a person who believed in the human race, a person who always gave everyone the benefit of the doubt. When she got slapped in the face by the universe, it had been her wakeup call. She'd seen what people could do, from the moment she witnessed Adan, the man who she sat beside at that very moment, end the life of a fellow human without hesitation. Without breaking a sweat.

She lived her life on standby mode. On the rare occasions, she'd have the house to herself, she would stay in the hallway where the front door was, on an oak chair with a shotgun by her leg reading a book. She would never let Adan see her. She knew she would get a whole lecture, which she really didn't want. She would wait for his car to leave the driveway and tiptoe to the front door. As the weeks passed, Adan began leaving less and less as he could see her reaction when he did come back home. She'd be jumpy and stutter on her words as if she'd bitten too much food to chew. She also walked as if she had two left feet.

Addison Sat on the red velvet couch in her room tightly gripping her hot cocoa mug, staring into the infinity of the crackling, warm and safe fire. Her feet were up on the couch under the fluffy midnight blue blanket. Her hair was tied up in an effortless bun, she'd taken off her makeup and revealed her freckles. Her back was supported by the armrest of the couch. It was mid-November and the chill outside frosted the window. Her attention was drawn to the window after noticing from the corner of her eye, white crystals of cloudy snow dropping from the sky. Her eyes widened and a huge smile stuck to her face. She let out a squeal of excitement. She placed her mug on the glass table by the couch and threw her blanket off her onto the carpet.

She got up and bounced her way to the window opening the curtain which reached the floor even more. Her mouth was left wide open as she watched the snowfall flake by flake. On the other side of the room, her door flung open to reveal a panicked Adan ready to fight. Addison wasn't bothered by the noise. She continued to stare. Adan's face dropped as he looked around to only see Addison staring out a window and jumping up and down.

"What the hell Addison?!" He said while walking past the fireplace and towards her.

Addison's face lit up like a little girl's as she turned around. Her smile was from eye to eye as she said, "It's snowing!"

Adan looked at her trying to figure her out for a long moment until he finally said "So? It always snows?" Adan looked puzzled.

His hair was all messy, and he wore grey sweatpants and a warm black hoodie. Addison began laughing and began "I'm going out." She walked straight passed him and through the door not even waiting up for him. Adan laughed and followed her. "Are you crazy? It's late and cold."

Addison ran out through the double doors from the kitchen and stood out in the snow which collected in her blond hair before slowly dissolving into water.

She lay down on the ground and began laughing while making snow Angels. Adan stood by the door and laughed at her while staring in adornment. He finally walked out into the snow and laid down beside her.

They both smiled and spoke using no words. "Every first snow, my grandfather would take me out, and we would stay out till midnight laughing and playing around. I remember one night, I slipped on a frozen puddle and landed on my arm, I spent the next three weeks in a cast, but it was so worth it." Addison had a way about her that made Adan freeze and want to do nothing but stare at her. Addison's smile slowly unraveled.

"Well if we're going to stay out here all night, I guess I should go get our jackets and make some hot cocoa." Adan brought back her smile and Addison added, "Extra whipped cream."

She held her smile until he walked back through those double doors. Her clothes were now wet, but she had no plans of moving. She sat with her hair on the wet grass and stared in the night sky.

She looked at those stars she could rarely see up in her apartment. Her eyes began to tear as she thought more of her grandfather. Her mind wound back to the night her mother told her about her grandfather.

It had been a night similar to this one. She was merely twelve years old. She'd come home to find her mother on the ground weeping. Her father was still at work and would be for the next few hours.

When she'd asked her mother what had happened, her mother wiped her tears away and pulled herself together. She sat Addison down at their small four-seater dining table in the kitchen and began telling her how her grandfather had had a heart attack while driving and died before doctors could do anything. They sat at that table and wept together for hours. Addison's cheeks began to stiffen from the cold tears. She sat up and wiped her tears and took a deep breath in.

She was startled by a loud ringing from her back pocket. She took out her phone and slid her finger forwards to answer. The caller had no idea, which made her a bit jumpy. She answered but no one spoke. All she could hear was heavy breathing. She said nothing and waited for them to say something. A deep familiar voice finally said. "I hope you've missed me as much as I have." Her heart froze in her chest and all her muscles tightened. In a panic, she began looking around her and rose to her feet like a scared cat.

"How the hell did you get this number?" She couldn't believe a word she heard.

"Why don't we play catch up over a cup of coffee?" Adan listened to the conversation, out of sight, tightly pressed against the wall of the house.

"What the hell do you want Alex? You fancy putting me in another building that you can blow up?" All the calmness she had gathered inside her over that the previous month dissolved like a cube of sugar in hot tea.

"So, we're keeping grudges? I thought so. How bout we try this another way."

Adan fought all temptation to grab the phone and let Alex know exactly what he felt about him, but he knew it would do no good.

Addison's hands began to shiver as Alex added "I've got your mother in a similar situation to yours, my advice is that you don't piss me off.

You come alone to the address I put in your mailbox last night and we can have a decent conversation or dearest mom gets to go swimming with the fish. It's up to you Adi, but just so you know, any funny business and I won't hesitate."

Before she could get any words in, he hung up leaving the phone dead. Adan dropped the coats in his hands and went rushing outside to find Addison completely still. He was afraid to try and move her, so he sat on the ground beside her and held her. He knew that was the only thing he could do for her at that moment.

"shh..." He said while running his hands through her soft hair. He pulled her in and let her rest her head on his chest. He warmed her with his safety and added. "I will find that bastard and make him wish he was never born. I promise you; we will figure it out."

His words should have calmed her down but instead, they agitated her. She pushed him away with all her strength and got up. She ran into the kitchen leaving Adan shouting her name. She looked around and found her white padded jacket on the floor along with Adan's a black leather jacket.

Adan got up and began walking towards the doors but before he could do anything to stop her, she closed the doors and locked him in.

"Addison! Addison stop!" He shouted at her as she walked away holding her jacket over her shoulder. She stood at the kitchen entry for a few moments staring at him and then it all clicked. She ran back towards the double doors and placed her hand on the cold class. Adan placed her hand where hers was and that was separating them was a piece of glass. They could feel each other's warmth through it.

"Adan..." She said while looking into his eyes and smiling. "I'm sorry, but I need to do this. This is my battle, not yours." Her eyes watered, but she managed to stop it as a tear balanced on her eyelash. Adan knew no words would stop her. If he'd learned anything about Addison over this past month was that when she was determined, nothing could stop her. Nothing could extinguish the fire in her eyes. Adan swallowed hard as if he'd just swallowed the twisted truth.

"Addison, I love you."

He looked her in the eyes and turned away. Addison wanted to say it back. That's all she wanted to do, but she knew if she opened her mouth to say one more word, she would let him come in and if she did that, he would stop her. She watched him and ran out of the kitchen. She ran up the stairs and got changed into a tight dark grey pencil skirt and a loose pink pastel blouse. She tucked it into her skirt. She put her hair into a messy bun with the occasional strands falling out and left the house. She walked down the long driveway and looked at the big house one last time admiring the dark grey brick and large modern windows one last time.

In the letterbox, she found a note, folded many times. In it was written the name of the park she and her grandfather would always play in before he died. She called a taxi which drove her to the entrance. It was around midnight and it was pitch dark outside, only the moonlight lit up some of the park's trees.

She walked down the familiar trail to reveal the cliff top she would sit on the edge of and makeup stories with him. She heard the exhaust of an idling car and knew exactly where he was. She walked through a clump of trees to reveal a clearing. This was the clearing where they had all their picnics. Addison had no time for memories as a car suddenly drove past gaining speed towards the cliff.

Her mother's velvet blue scarf stuck in the left door.

A car her mother was in, heading straight towards the edge of that cliff. Addison ran as fast as her legs would go and managed to catch the door handle. She ripped the door open and jumped into the driver seat.

The car was quickly gathering speed, getting closer and closer to the edge of the cliff, she looked frantically around but couldn't see her mother anywhere. She'd been tricked and that wasn't even the worst part. She'd stupidly fallen into another of his traps.

Out the windscreen she saw the edge of the cliff moving closer to the front of the car. She knew she couldn't jump out. It was too late. Many people say near-death experiences cause your life to flash before her eyes. Thoughts flashed through her mind. A memory of the last time she'd seen her grandfather appeared in her mind. They sat in the clearing she'd seen not too long ago on a red and white checkered blanket with a picnic basket.

Her grandfather had a smug look on his face. "So, since it's your birthday soon and I have to be away on business I thought I would give you your gift early."

Addison's face lit up as she said, "Soon? My birthdays in January and it's November." Addison began to giggle at him.

He went through the picnic basket and pulled out a black box and handed it to her. As she opened the box to reveal a red velvet inside her eyes lit up at the beautiful neckless which had been so perfectly placed. "Grandpa, you didn't have to." She said in awe.

There was Addison more than fourteen years later in a situation she'd never pictured herself to be in. She ran her fingers along her chest where that necklace had kept its place for so long. She closed her eyes and came to peace with the fact that this was it. She was at peace until she remembered the man she'd left to get here. She regretted only one thing. She regretted not opening her mouth. She regretted not saying it back and letting him in. She regretted not being able to feel him near her, to feel his warm breath on her face as he spoke or feeling his lips on her one last time.

She whispered underneath her breath the words she'd chosen to be her last.

"I love you too Adan Gibbons." She swallowed hard and looked at the close getting closer and closer. She closed her eyes and held her breath. Felling no regrets any more. She was fully at peace.

Adan knew for a fact there was no way to stop Addison from leaving to go after her mother. However, Adan was not a stupid man. He knew that if he beat Addison to it, he could get out the yard and get into one of his cars. He would follow the car she was in and be there just in case she got into trouble, which he knew was guaranteed if Alex was around. As he sat in the car and waited for Addison to walk out those front doors, his mind began to trail back a few years.

His mother died when he was born and it had been just him and his father until his father got sick and had gone off to join his mother. From the age of six, he'd been living on the cold, damp streets of London fighting for his life until one day, exactly nineteen years ago, three months and twenty-nine days ago, he was caught in the act. He'd taken exactly twenty pounds and fifty-three pence.

He was eleven and had taught himself how to be an excellent pickpocket. He'd never been caught before. As he reached for the purse of the woman in front him, his hand was slapped away by the man beside him. When he looked up, he saw a man in a black suit and white button-up shirt with blond hair and bright blue eyes towering over him with a smirk on his face. Ever since then he learned he would never have to be alone. He learned everything he knew from this man. He learned how to switch off his emotions. He learned how to kill, and he learned how not to hurt inside. The man flew him back to New York, where he was taken in and raised by the man who he best known as Stephan Willmar. Stephan Willmar was the leader of one of the top gangs which ruled New York.

They were called "The Lions" as in the kings of the jungle, the ones who all feared. They raised him as their own. Adan's memories were blurred out at the sight of Addison which left him shocked. She wasn't going to fight. She was dressed up. She was going to play along with his game. She got into a cab and Adan followed close behind.

Addison sat in that car; she'd said the only words she wanted to as her last. She closed her eyes and held her breath only to hear three gunshots. The car halted, centimeters away from the edge of the cliff. She opened her bright blue eyes and looked around catching her breath. Out of the nearby bushes, Adan walked over to the door and placed his hand on the handle, gun in hand. The Adan Addison knew was not the same man that stood in front of her. This man had the same look in his eyes as the ruthless killer Addison had bumped into what now seemed a lifetime ago.

She wasn't sure if she should be mad or scared. She kept her mouth shut and watched Adan's grey eyes scan her for injuries before pulling the door open. He looked cold, he looked dead inside. He looked like a man sane people would avoid. Addison gasped as he opened the door and lifted her out the car. He walked uphill, away from the cliff's end with her in his arms and dumped her unceremoniously onto the ground.

Chapter 9

"What the hell were you thinking?!" He shouted at her and stopped mid-sentence as he saw the face of the man, he resented most in this world. Alex. "Guess she couldn't stay away from me.

"Alex's voice was deep and sharp like a knife-edge. Addison rose to her feet and tried to stand beside Adan only for him to push her behind him. Adan said nothing. No words could possibly express his feelings towards Alex. Keeping one hand behind his back to make sure Addison didn't follow him, he took a step towards Alex, not taking his eyes off him. Alex began walking towards Adan with a twisted smile.

"You don't need her, wasn't he enough?" Adan said coldly.

Alex laughed and said, "Enough?!"

He laughed some more and added, "I will eliminate his entire bloodline for what he did to my father." Alex's smile faded.

Adan move liked lightning, punching Alex so hard he crumpled backwards onto the ground and lay there unmoving. One final kick to the temple made sure.

"What was he talking about? Who's a bloodline?" She tried to hide the fear in her voice but the voice crack revealed it. Adan tried to touch her hand, but she pulled it away.

Adan's face began to relax and warm up. "I have a lot to tell you but right now, we need to get away, he for sure isn't alone." Adan put his hand out and Addison grabbed it. They began running into the woods without looking around. They ran until the trail brought them out onto a small road surrounded by trees and bushes.

A road looking similar to the one where Adan's car was parked when Addison waited for Nico. Adan lifted up his leather jacket and took a gun and threw it to her. Addison caught it and looked at it as if it were some type of alien. "Why?" She asked while looking down at it. "Just in case." Adan said right before he winked. They both started walking down the road.

They found a bus stop on the pavement and sat down on the wooden, broken down, bench.

"That was purely idiotic, do you have a death wish?!" Adan's voice was tense and strong, but not loud. Addison looked down at her feet and bit her tongue. She had so many questions. So many answers that she needed. Adan stood up and stood in front of her, telling her over and over how stupid it was, how she needs to be more careful.

"Stop!" She shouted covering her ears. "Enough is enough!" Her voice was getting louder and stronger with every word and this brought a smile to his face. Some sort of twisted, wicked satisfaction. Addison stood up and was now close enough to him to either kiss him or hit him. She did neither. She'd learned a few things from him along with fighting. She'd learned how to keep a poker face, to bury her emotions deep down.

"What was Alex talking about when he said his bloodline?" She stepped back.

"Your grandfather's." Adan's tough-guy act weakened as his instinctive defense weakened.

There was something about him that was softer, calmer and dare she say, nicer. Addison said nothing, so he took it as his cue to continue.

"He wasn't who you thought." His words faded into the night's silence. Addison could hear but couldn't register. She could see his mouth moving but couldn't understand his words. "He killed Alex's father", his words blurred again. "Alex then killed him and then..." Addison stood up, pointed her weapon at the sky and pulled the trigger over and over, her hand tightening on the grip as it cut into her hand transferring all her built-up anger into the bullets tearing out of the barrel of the gun. She'd lost control.

The anger, the betrayal and confusion had infused her body and had taken control of the gun she held so tightly in her hand. She stood there tense and frozen but shooting continuously. The bullets spun through the air leaving the acrid smell of the burning propellent swirling around her head. Addison's face was stiff and her eyes were dim and half-closed. Adan stepped aside, but he knew trying to stop her would be madness, and she needed to get it out.

Something in her clicked as he suddenly regained control over herself. As the world came back to her, she noticed a movement in her peripheral vision. One of Alex's men had followed them through the woods and was about to take a shot at Adan. Her instincts kicked in and took control. Every part in her body wanted to deny what she had just done but the gun in her hand was part of her. Instinctively, the gun raised and pointed at the figure crouched at the edge of the clearing. Her grip tightening slightly and the sights lined up.

BANG, BANG, BANG! Three bullets danced through the air into the center of the crouching figure, followed by the thud as his lifeless body hit the cold, indifferent ground. Adan stood across from her smiling as he knew she was the true granddaughter of Stephan Willmar. What he didn't know was that this moment, this memory of killing would haunt her forever.

The heavy gun slipped out of her soft hands like sand running through her fingers. The air around her turned black, stiff and heavy as she realized what she had just done. She drew her attention from the body she had just turned into a corpse to meet his eyes.

"You! You did this! You made me this monster!" Addison's voice echoed through the cold, dark street as she stood above a pool of blood. Hurt and afraid of herself.

He stood across from her. His face was stiff. Talking to him was like talking to a brick wall. His blood-chilling grey eyes looked at her but stared straight through her. His curly black hair fell perfectly in front of his eyes, highlighting the occasional sparkle that made its way into his eyes.

He had a permanent smirk stitched onto his face. Addison wore a dark grey pencil skirt with a pastel pink blouse hanging loosely. Her warm blond hair gathered into a messy bun which was now falling apart. Her sparkling, honest, blue eyes were now cloudy and lifeless. Her freckle painted cheeks were now tear-stained.

"Why?! Why couldn't you just leave me be? Why couldn't you just have turned away?!" Her voice that usually sounded like sweet honey was now bitter and cold. Her mascara had stained her tears black.

He took his hand out of his ripped black jeans and took off his leather jacket while moving close enough to Addison to make her lose her breath. He brushed her hair out of her face and placed his heavy jacket on her shoulders. Addison attempted to speak, but she was at a loss of words.

He stepped back and said in a matter of fact voice, "No point crying over spilt milk." Then silence came.

He then moved his hand over to her face and wiped her tears. Enraged Addison pushed him back. His smirk remained plastered onto his perfectly chiseled face. She pushed again and again, but he wouldn't move. She lifted her arms and attempted to punch him, but she was blocked by his arms catching hers.

"After everything, I don't know why I stay, I don't know why I don't just turn you in right now." Her voice breaking more with every word.

"I don't know why I don't just shoot you and end it all right here." Her tears weren't tears of sadness any more.

He leaned down and picked up the gun from the ground and wiped off the blood. "Here you go" He handed her the loaded gun.

"Lucky you, one bullet left." His smirk grew greater than before.

He looked straight into her eyes. His eyes were on her and her eyes were on him. She took the gun from him and in a blink, raised it and fired. One final BANG! The bullet moved past Adan's head as if he had an invisible shield. Adan turned his head and followed the bullet like a cat following a laser. The bullet continued straight across the clearing, passing straight through the chest of the sniper couched out of sight in the undergrowth, his weapon tumbling to the ground. Adan's smile faded as he turned to look at Addison. He tried to speak but the words wouldn't come out.

"I know..." She said, while putting one hand on his shoulder, running through his hair. She kissed him, and he held her and together they enjoyed the last moment before all hell really broke loose. Adan shuddered in her arms and his knees thudded into the cold bloody ground. Addison instinctively jumped back. She could have spent a lifetime preparing for that moment and still she wouldn't have been ready.

Adan looked up at Addison puzzled, his hands moving over to his chest. Blood had begun flowing out between his fingers.

Addison quickly moved over to him. He looked innocent, like a little child who'd been denied another candy. He was badly hurt and you could see it on his stiff, weakening face.

"Adan!" She pressed her hands over his to try and stop the gushing blood. She was trying to stop a flooding sink with a glass. She put her head next to his and looked him in the eyes. He opened his mouth again; his lips were dry and cold as she kissed him to stop him speaking.

"Don't you dare speak. Don't you dare say goodbye." Her voice cracked and her eyes watered again.

He touched her face leaving a bloody trail behind his touch.

"Addison, I'm so sorry I didn't tell you about your grandfather. I'm sorry I couldn't keep my promise to him and keep you safe."

His cloudy grey eyes closed slowly and his mouth relaxed along with every part of his body. Addison stood there for a moment trying to process the train that just hit her. She kept a hand on top of his wound which had stained his shirt red and stroked his face with her thumb.

"No, you don't get to say sorry. You don't get to be sorry because you have all our lives to make it up to me. You don't get to leave."

She stared at him hoping her words were magical and would wake him up, she added. "Please."

Her voice getting softer and weaker with every cry.

"It's me and you against the world."

She placed her face on his chest not caring about the blood and sobbed. One final bullet danced its way through the cold November air and embedded itself in her back. Addison gasped and felt unable to move. Her vision began darkening around the edges of her eyes. At that moment even the moon itself was too afraid to see what came next. The clouds moved over the moon and all light faded along with Addison's, soft sweet voice.

The darkness was lit up by the blue and red lights and the silence disturbed by the loud echoing sirens. Addison closed her eyes and smiled. She was finally going to be in his arms. Her hearing slowly began to fade until there was only silence and pitch blackness. The words she'd said played over and over in her head, "It's me and you against the world"

Chapter 10

All the light faded and suddenly Addison was back in her childhood bedroom. She looked up at the pink walls and admired all her finger paintings. Her white door opened and her grandfather walked in and sat on the chair by her bed.

He smiled at her and said, "You met Adan."

"I sure did." She said while smiling. All she wanted to do was cry her eyes out but all she could do was smile.

"Ever since I assigned him to you, I told him to protect you from afar, to never reveal his identity." Stephan gave himself a smile of acknowledgement and added on, "He never did follow orders. Always doing his own thing that one."

He stood up from the chair and went over to hug Addison. "Have you ever heard of the Lions?" He said.

Addison raised an eyebrow and said, "The gang who terrorized New York?"

"I wouldn't say terrorized, I'd say protected." He smiled and added on, "There were two gangs, two kingdoms if you may, who rivalled against each other for as long as they could remember. After your mother was born, your grandmother's break lines were cut and her car spun out of control and off a bridge. I made it my life's quest to take down Monique, the leader of the other gang. Once I did, his gang spent all their time trying to kill me. One day, when I was in London to go and visit Adan. My break lines were cut too and the last man I'd seen in my hospital room was Alex dressed as a nurse. He'd injected something into my IV bag and the rest was, well history."

Addison kept her smile and said, "For that reason, he's coming after your bloodline?"

Stephan nodded and said, "All I wanted to say was, don't ever be afraid, I am right here always."

Addison shook off his words and got up from her bed. "I'm going to kill him. I'm going to hurt him so badly." She was enraged and furious.

She calmed herself and added "So the little boy in the picture I found was Adan?"

Stephan smiled.

"Darling, sit back down I have one more thing to say." She sat down and listened as words came out of his mouth.

"Congratulations."

Her vision morphed back into reality with his words in her head as the light of the world came back.

Addison lay in a hard hospital bed, surrounded by a group of doctors, all talking about different things, at once. Her head was pounding.

One of the doctors who had fiery red hair and green eyes came over to her and said quietly "Hi

Addison." Her voice made the whole room quiet. Addison knew she'd been shot but she had no concern about herself.

"Adan?" She asked. Her words came out all muddled up. The doctor looked away from Addison and over to another doctor.

"Addison, you were shot in the back, you were very lucky as we were able to get the bullet out without causing any spinal damage. The bullet only hit flesh." Addison stared at the doctor and said nothing. She ripped the IV from her arm and detached all of the monitor leads. The machine behind her began beeping wildly.

"Thank you so much for taking care of me but I really have to go. "She sat up straight but the doctors managed to push her back down onto the bed.

"Please Addison wait, there's more..." Before the doctor could continue, Addison interrupted.

"I don't think you understand. Get your hands off me and help me off this bed. I need to find Adan." Her voice was harsh and fed up.

"Addison you are 7 weeks pregnant." The doctor said removing her hands from Addison.

The world froze and Addison pieced the information together. Her grandfather knew. She looked the doctor in the eye, took a deep breath and asked. "Is it okay?"

The doctor smiled and reassured her, "Your baby is perfectly healthy."

The news hit her like a brick in the face, she was going to be a mother? She looked from side to side of her bed and around her hospital room. She then remembered Adan. There was no way she could be a mother without him.

"Adan, where is Adan?" All the doctors looked at one and other and then back at Addison.

"Is Adan the man you were with?" the doctor asked, still not completely looking at Addison.

"No, he's that pig flying outside the window. Yes, he's the man I came in with, where is he?!"

"Addison, he lost a lot of blood, his brain was deprived of oxygen for too long. I'm afraid he may not wake up." The doctor tried to sooth Addison, but she just angered her. Addison put her feet on the cold floor.

"Where is he?" She'd had enough of everyone tiptoeing around the truth.

The doctors kept silent. "Where the hell is, he?!" Her voice was loud and shook through her body.

"ADAN!" she shouted.

The doctors ran over to her and tried to calm her down, but she wasn't having it. She began to fight and punch until finally she was lifted off the ground and into her bed. "You can't do this." The woman said.

"The hell I can!" Addison corrected.

"You're going to tear your sutures and hurt your baby, now I strongly suggest you calm down and we will get you a wheelchair and take you to his room."

Addison calmed down and took a deep breath in. Some nurses came in and reattached her EKG monitors. The machine behind her began beating. Her plan was to go over there and wake him up from the wicked spell placed on him. She would kiss him, and they would live happily ever after.

She grabbed the doctor's hands and said, "Listen to me, I love that man too much to lose him. Promise me you will do everything, take the most extreme measures to make sure he lives. To make sure this baby has a father."

The doctor swallowed hard and said, "Addison he's in very bad..." The doctor was interrupted by Addison cold harsh words, "Promise me, you will keep him alive!" She said intensely.

The doctor grabbed her hand back from Addison and looked at her before walking out of the room.

"Me and you against the world." She muttered under her breath.

Chapter 11

This part will be written in Addison's point of view.

Addison:

I sat in the hard, cold, uncomfortable bed anxiously waiting for anyone to walk through that room and take me to him. I wasn't done with him. I wasn't ready to let him go. I watched the outside world move on without me through the small window in my wooden door. The machine behind me kept beeping. I moved my hand onto my stomach and began to think of Adan. What if he does die? What if I need to raise this baby by telling It, its father died at the hands of an angry man? My head hurt just at the idea.

My mind began wandering back to the first time we met. I was so different back then. I remember being frozen by his ice-cold gaze. He was perfect.

Even after I saw him murder that man, I still couldn't look away. When I ducked behind that wall and saw a bullet hit the wall next to me, I freaked out. Then I remembered how I punched Alex and began laughing.

As I was laughing, the door swung open and the red-haired doctor came in with a wheelchair behind her. The excitement on my face must have been obvious as the doctor began smiling back. She disconnected me from the machines and hung my IV bag onto the wheelchair.

"Are you ready?" She asked me a question I had no idea how to answer. She then began telling me what to expect. As we went through the cold hallways, I saw all the ICU units pass in a blur. So many families were grieving.

As soon as I saw Adan, I would tell him he has to wake up, and he would. I began day dreaming of all the memories we've shared together. The first time he kissed me, my whole world stopped. All my fears faded and all my worries disappeared. I felt safe and at home in his arms.

That night when I thought I lost him in that building, I didn't give up on him. I fought and turned every stone and, in the end, he was still the one to find me.

He changed me for the better. He made me happy. He made me confident and most of all he taught me how to love. Because of him, I could smile, because of him, I laughed. He gave a gift I couldn't have dreamed of. He gave me motherhood.

The first time he put me in that ring and made me punch him, even though I knew he was so strong, I was afraid I'd hurt him. My happiest moments were those late nights we would stay by the fireplace, I would fall asleep in his arms. He would carry me to my bed and tuck me in while I was asleep. He may have been a ruthless killer, he may have harmed people with no hesitation, but to me he was good. He cared for me. He loved me. I never said it back to him. He's never heard me say it.

We got into that fight. When he handed me the gun, it killed me, but I'm pretty sure I was going to shoot him. When I saw that man about to fire a bullet into him, I snapped.

The fight was irrelevant, I shot the man without thinking. I kissed him and then he fell to the ground. So many thoughts rushed through my mind. I've never felt this way about anyone. I held him. I watched him draw his last breath of cold dry air that night. I was the one who heard his last words fade into the night. My hands were so full of his blood. There was blood everywhere. Then came the stinging pain in my back. If I hadn't made it, at least I would have been in his arms.

I didn't realize my eyes were watering. The doctor awoke me from my trance. "We're here."

I took a deep breath in and stood up from my wheelchair. He was in a room identical to mine. There were hundreds of tubes and needles stuck in him. There must have been seven monitors all synchronized and beeping. I sat down on the cream leatherette chair beside his bed and watched him. His hair was still curly and fell in front of his eyes. There was a tube down his throat breathing for him. I held his hand and fought every tear back. "Hey, you!" I said to him and swallowed down all the tears. I had no idea what to say and where to start. My eyes watered but I knew I couldn't cry. Not in front of him. I had to be strong.

"You're so silly." I stood up and moved a piece of hair out of his face. His skin was pale and his lips were dry.

"I guess this is the part where I tell you that you're going to be a dad." I managed to keep a smile on my face. I watched his face and all of a sudden, I could swear I saw him smile, it was only for a few seconds, imperceptible but I knew he did.

It was his iconic smirk. I squeezed his hand. "I love you too." I said and began sobbing.

"I'm so sorry. Please, please don't make me raise this baby alone. Don't make me tell it I watched you die in my arms. Please Adan please come back." I tried to stop myself from crying but I couldn't.

The machines behind him began beeping less and less until they started blaring. The line went flat. Teams of doctors ran in and from all corners, you could hear. "Get a crash cart."

"Get her out of here" I stayed in that chair holding his hand until I was carried away screaming "You promised!"

As soon as they took me out of the room, I fell onto the floor weeping.

"Adan!" I didn't want to move. I couldn't move. I would stay by his side. From inside the room, you could hear. "3,2,1 clear." The same words repeated over and over for the next half an hour.

I sat on the floor, frozen in my spot. People passed and stared but I didn't care. When the doctors came out of the room their mouths

134

moved but no words came out. I stood up and pushed past them. I ran into his room and saw his cold body turning blue. His eyes were closed and his bed was completely flat. All the machines were screaming. I turned to the door where doctors were watching me and screamed at them, "Help him!" They stood there and didn't move.

"Help him! Do your job and help him. You can't just leave him." The doctor with the red hair came in and gave me a sympathetic smile and began explaining to me how his brain had stopped which stopped his heart. There was nothing they could do. She walked over to his bed and covered his face. "Time of death, 05:23 am." She walked back over to me and said. "I'm sorry for your loss" and walked out.

I stayed in that room for hours. I sat in that chair and replayed every moment we've ever had together.

"Adan, please."

"Adan, I love you!"

Just like that the man I loved. The father of my baby was dead, and he'd left behind his lifeless corpse. From that day on, I promised myself I would never love another man again.

Them:

They say you don't miss what you have until it's gone. Addison had no idea how lucky she was to have had a man like Adan in her life.

Months passed since his death and Addison went back home to live with her mother who now looks after her. She now sleeps in her childhood room which was pink but is painted over with a creamy white color. The room across from hers was the guest room which her mother had turned into the baby's nursery. Addison spent most of her time inside that house only going out to doctors' appointments. She would rarely come out of her room and would eat every meal there.

Her mother knew that she couldn't say anything. She had every right to do this. The months flew past like leaves in the autumn breeze, the day Addison would get to meet her baby grew closer and closer. The date was the twenty-fourth of June.

Addison laid asleep in a familiar hospital bed with three pillows holding up her head. She wore a hospital gown with printed blue squares. The sun rays coming in through the partly closed blinds made her spread out hair look like golden strands. Her mother watching her sleep while knitting a hat out of pastel yellow wool.

The wooden hospital door with the window at the top of it gently opened and screeched against the cold white tiled floor. The nurse wore bright pink scrubs. She was wheeling a small, plastic, see-through bed with white covers. The nurse pushed the bed all the way into the room and parked it right near her bed.

Inside the bed was a little baby, swaddled into a white blanket with a blue and pink bird pattern. The baby had a tiny button nose and a few locks of dark blond hair. It had perfect little rounded ears and the sweetest, gentlest lips which looked as if they were drawn on. The baby had full, doll-like eyes which were grey but turned blue in the sun. The baby's bed was wrapped in a pink ribbon with a big bow on the side. There was a sign attached to the bed which read; 'I'm a Girl!'

Addison's mother Silvia stood up from the chair and rushed towards the little bed. She gave a grateful smile to the nurse and picked up the baby. "She's perfect." She said in awe while keeping her voice down. The baby began to cackle and woke up Addison. The first thing Addison did was look down at her stomach. "What the?!" She began to panic but saw her mother holding the cutest most precious baby in the world.

Addison's eyes began to water as she swallowed hard. "Is that?" The baby began crying and Silvia gently placed her in Addison's arms. She held her baby and began to sway her back and forth. Addison began sobbing and finally said, "Hey baby girl." Her voice cracking. Her mother smiled and kissed Addison on the forehead. "I'm going to go see if I can get you something to eat."

Addison agreed without taking her eyes off the little bundle of joy in her hands.

"Hi, baby." She said to the little girls in her arms in a soft voice. The baby's eyes closed and Addison added on, "Your Daddy would have been freaking out so much right now, he'd be overjoyed with excitement to meet you. If he were here right now, he'd have his signature smirk on." She took a pause and took a deep breath in. This was the first time she'd spoken about Adan without crying. "Your daddy may have been a scary man to others. He was feared by many but that was only because people couldn't understand him and his story." She tapped the little baby's nose. "Aren't you just so gorgeous. You have his eyes. You have my lips and I hope you get his hair. He had amazing hair. He also had an amazing laugh, just like yours." She said while tickling the baby and listening to her hypnotizing giggles.

All the tears she'd shed over the past few months didn't matter anymore. It was all worth it. Every single part of it. Addison looked over at the baby bed, which had no name on it. "I need to give you a name, don't I?" Addison looked around and then back at her face. "Rose," she whispered under her breath. "Beautiful but full of thorns." Addison could have sworn she felt a familiar touch on her shoulder as if Adan was in the room beside her. "You're my little Rosie." Addison smiled and felt calm for the first time in what felt forever. "And every time my little Rosie gets upset at the world or whenever you feel like giving up, I will tell you exactly what your father would tell me. It's me and you against the world. I love you so much." Addison promised to herself that she would die before anyone touched her little Rosie.

Her loss was a great one, but this little life in her hands made it hurt just a bit less. Addison wanted to raise her daughter in London, the same place her father had grown up. She knew she had a whole new journey ahead of her, but she was ready to take the first step into her new story. But that was for later.

Right now, she would treasure this first moment of many others she gets to spend with her daughter who was the spitting image of Adan. "It's me and you against the world." Her voice faded and morphed into Adan's. His voice echoed off the walls. Every day since he died, she woke up and wished it had all been a dream. However, this day, in that moment, if it had been a dream, she wished she would never wake up. There was a knock at her door, expecting it to be her mother, she said, "Come in."

A young man walked in with a bouquet of flowers and placed them on her night stand and walked without saying a word. With one hand Addison retrieved the small note buried in between the floors.

The note read,

Congratulations.

-Alex

Just like that, her bubble of joy and safety burst.